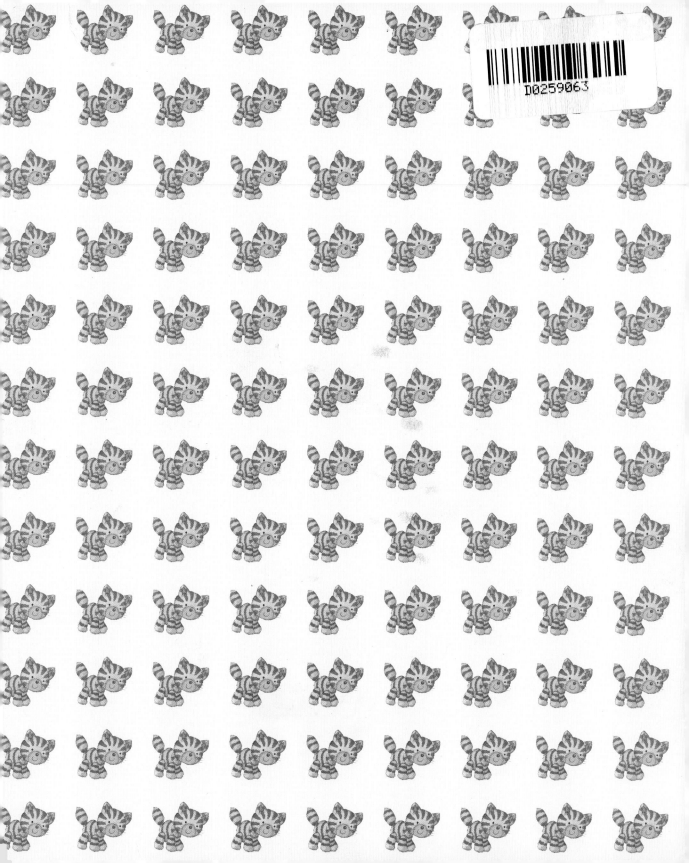

Stories by Maureen Spurgeon
Illustrated by Gill Guile & Stephen Holmes

This edition first published 2003 by Brown Watson
The Old Mill, 76 Fleckney Road,
Kibworth Beauchamp, Leics LE8 0HG

ISBN: 0-7097-1581-7

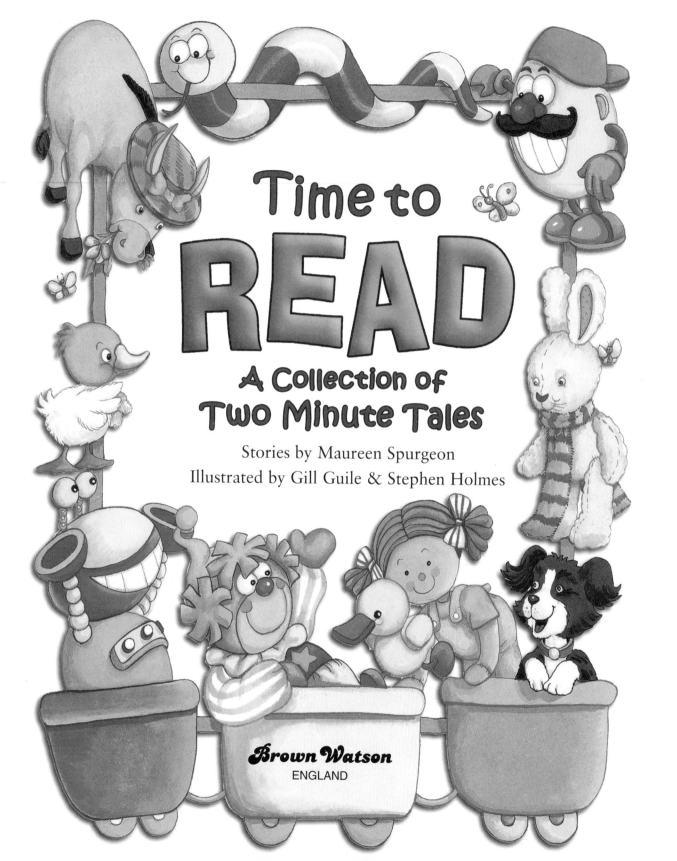

Time to READ

A Collection of Two Minute Tales

Stories by Maureen Spurgeon

Illustrated by Gill Guile & Stephen Holmes

Brown Watson

ENGLAND

CONTENTS

Page No.

DONNY GOES TO HOSPITAL

'Woof-woof!' barked Dinky Dog. 'Someone is at the gate!'

'Quiet, Dinky!' said the farmer. 'It is only Nurse from the hospital!'

'We want Donny at the hospital at one o'clock,' Nurse told the farmer. 'We shall look after him!'

Dinky could not believe it!

'Poor Donny Donkey!' she said to Hector Horse. 'Farmer says he is going to hospital, today!'

'What?' Hector could not believe it! 'We must find him!'

'There he is!' barked Dinky. 'In the field, with Brad and Mary!'

'Let us put these reins on you,' Brad was saying. 'Then we will take you to hospital, Donny!'

'Woof!' barked Dinky. 'Then I am going to the hospital, too! Donny is my friend!'

Mary understood. 'All right, Dinky!' she said. 'You can come with us!'

Dinky worried all the way to the hospital. But Donny plodded on, as if he could not wait to be there!

'This way, Donny!' said Nurse.

She led the way into a garden, with balloons hanging around. There was an ice cream van and a lucky dip stall and people playing games and winning prizes.

'Welcome to our hospital garden party!' said Nurse. 'Now, who will be first to have a donkey ride?'

All afternoon, Donny enjoyed giving rides to the children and being the star of the garden party.

And Dinky Dog? She still could not believe it!

READ THESE WORDS AGAIN!

could believe
reins friend
understood come
worried plodded
could wait
garden lucky
prizes party

14

'What was that?' said Dolly.

'It is Windmill Man!' said Baby Bear. 'Look! The wind is blowing him higher and higher!'

'What can we do?' cried Fairy.

'Unwind my string!' said Kite. 'Slide me through the window!'

So the toys unwound the string and slid Kite through the window. As they let out his string, he flew higher and higher.

'Windmill Man!' Kite shouted. 'I will fly as near to you as I can! You must get hold of my string!'

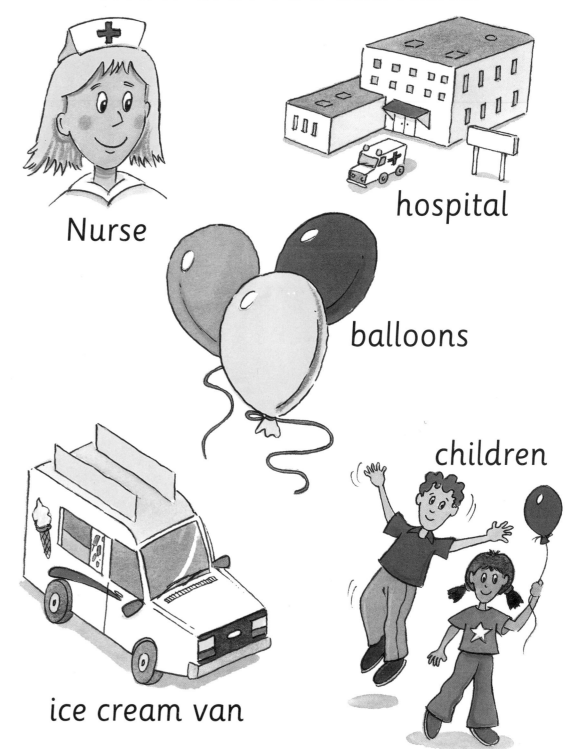

WHAT CAN YOU SEE HERE?

Nurse

hospital

balloons

children

ice cream van

KITE TO THE RESCUE!

The toys called him Windmill Man. He was fixed to the garden fence, winding a wheel. The more the wind blew, the faster Windmill Man wound his wheel.

One day, a strong wind began to blow. Indoors, it rattled the doors and shook the windows. Outside, it howled across the garden.

There was a loud CRACK and Windmill Man broke away from the fence! Up into the air he went, his wheel banging on the window.

Windmill Man reached out bravely. How he grabbed Kite's string he never knew. But he did.

'Clever Kite has done it!' shouted Spaceman. 'Pull in the string, Robot!'

The more they pulled the string, the closer Kite and Windmill Man came. At last, they squeezed in through the window together.

'What a rescue!' said Windmill Man. 'Thank you, Kite!'

'Thank YOU, Windmill Man!' said Kite. 'I have always wanted to fly in a really strong wind!'

READ THESE WORDS AGAIN!

fixed winding
wheel wind
wound strong
howled broke
unwind slide
closer through
rescue really

WHAT CAN YOU SEE HERE?

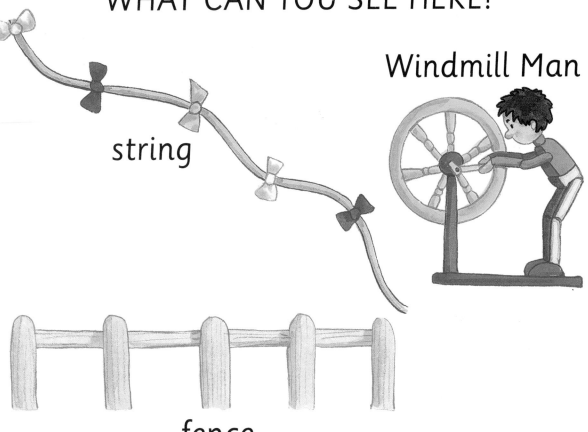

string

Windmill Man

fence

window

door

A DRAGON ON THE FARM!

One day, Cora Cow was at the stream. Suddenly two big, round eyes stared up at her.

'Moo!' went Cora. 'A dragon!' She ran away in fright!

'Baa!' went Letty Lamb. 'What is wrong, Cora Cow?'

'There – there is a dragon in the stream!' stammered Cora. 'With eyes as big as – as marbles!'

Letty looked into the stream. Two big, round eyes stared up at her! Green claws stretched out!

Letty and Cora ran away in fright!

'Hey!' went Guppy Goat. 'What is wrong, Letty and Cora?'

'There – there is a dragon in the stream!' stammered Cora. 'With eyes as big as – as saucers!'

'And green claws, as long as – as snakes!' cried Letty.

Guppy looked into the stream. Two big, round eyes stared up at him! Green claws stretched out. Long legs waved about! Guppy, Letty and Cora ran away in fright!

'What is wrong?' said Pixie Puppy.

'There is a dragon in the stream!' said Guppy. 'With claws like a – a tiger!'

'Legs like – like a monster!' added Letty.

'And eyes as big as – as wheels!' ended Cora Cow.

Pixie went to see. Two big eyes stared up at her. Claws stretched out. Long green legs waved about.

'A dragon?' she barked. 'Ha-ha! It is only a little FROG!'

'Well!' said Cora. 'NOW we can all have a nice drink of water!'

READ THESE WORDS AGAIN!

stream	eyes
fright	stared
stretched	claws
tiger	monster
wheels	green
about	barked
little	nice

WHAT CAN YOU SEE HERE?

marbles

dragon

saucers

snakes

frog

BLUE RABBIT STAYS OUT!

It had been a long, hot day. The toys had been out in the garden.

'Time to go indoors!' said Dolly.

'It is too hot to go indoors,' said Blue Rabbit. 'I shall stay here!' And he hid behind the rose bush!

'Where is Blue Rabbit?' someone was saying.

'In the toy box, I expect,' said another voice. 'Let us go indoors!'

The door closed. After that, it grew dark very quickly. The moon cast strange shadows.

Soon, the wind began to blow. Blue Rabbit wished he felt braver!

He trod on something slimy! Ugh! It was a worm, slithering down into a hole in the ground!

'Silly me!' said Blue Rabbit. 'I... I... what was that?' He had heard the patter of paws. Two pointed ears and a pointed nose appeared.

'A fox!' cried Blue Rabbit. 'Oh, p-p-please do not eat me!' But Fox did not want to eat a toy rabbit!

'Miaow!' went the cat. She picked Blue Rabbit up carefully in her mouth!

She carried him to the cat-flap!

'I am not one of your kittens!' he cried. 'Put me down!'

By the time they got inside the cat-flap, Blue Rabbit was so tired. He closed his eyes...

'Another fine day!' said a voice. 'And, here is Blue Rabbit, all ready to go into the garden!'

Blue Rabbit blinked. Had he really been carried by a cat, scared by a worm and chased by a fox?

'No...' he told himself. 'I must have sat in the sun for too long!'

READ THESE WORDS AGAIN!

garden	indoors
someone	saying
closed	quickly
strange	wished
braver	slithering
pointed	appeared
carried	tired
blinked	chased

WHAT CAN YOU SEE HERE?

fox

Blue Rabbit

rose bush

cat-flap

shadows

THE STORY OF THE MILK CHURN

'I shall throw away this old milk churn!' said the farmer's wife. She put it outside the dairy.

The stable-girl was loaded down with hay for Hector Horse. She was glad to see the churn! 'Just the thing to carry the hay!' she said.

She carried it to the stables. Then she emptied it and put it outside.

The farrier had just put some new horseshoes on Hector, when the handle of his tool-bag broke! He was glad to see the milk churn!

'Just the thing to carry my tools!' he said. The farrier rolled the churn full of tools to his car. He put the tools in the boot and left the churn by the gate.

Along came the farmer with a sack of cattle-feed. He was glad to see the milk churn! 'Just the thing to carry this cattle-feed!' he said.

He emptied the cattle-feed into the churn and took it to the cowshed. He emptied the feed into a manger for the cows to eat and left the churn outside.

The churn was under a big tree. It was full of fallen leaves when Brad and Mary found it next day!

'What a nice lot of fallen leaves to take to school!' cried Mary.

They carried the milk churn to the farmhouse. Then they emptied the leaves into a bag and left the churn outside.

'So much junk to get rid of!' said their Mum. She was glad to see the milk churn! 'I am glad I did not throw this old churn away!' she said. 'It is MUCH too useful!'

READ THESE WORDS AGAIN!

thing	carry
carried	stables
emptied	handle
broke	tools
boot	gate
cattle	fallen
leaves	useful

WHAT CAN YOU SEE HERE?

farrier

milk churn

horseshoes

tools

manger

CLOWN AND MONKEY

Clown did like making the toys laugh. He could pull funny faces. He could do funny tricks. And now he was trying to juggle!

'Struggling to do juggling!' he said, as a ball hit him on his nose. BUMP! How the toys laughed!

'I can juggle!' said Monkey. 'And I can throw the balls much higher than you, Clown!'

'Show us, then!' cried Robot.

So Monkey went and stood beside Clown.

'Catch!' said Clown. He threw some balls to Monkey. One, two, three!

'See?' said Monkey. 'I can keep all the balls in the air, without dropping any! One, two, three!'

The toys clapped and cheered.

'Throw me another ball!' cried Monkey. 'And another!'

'One!' He threw a ball up high.

'Two!' He threw another. 'Three! Four! And another! And another! I am juggling with five balls!'

'Monkey,' began Clown, 'wait...'

But Monkey was too pleased with himself to wait for anything!

'Now for the finish!' he cried. 'I catch one ball! Two! Three! Four... and six! Do you think I am the greatest juggler, ever?'

'No!' cried the toys, as the SIXTH ball crashed down on Monkey's head. 'You cannot count, Monkey!'

'But you are still a fine juggler,' said Clown with a smile. 'And you made the toys laugh even louder than I did!'

READ THESE WORDS AGAIN!

laugh   funny
could   juggle
struggling   higher
stood   beside
catch   without
threw   air
cheered   count

54

WHAT CAN YOU SEE HERE?

funny faces

one ball

juggler

six balls

monkey

HECTOR AND THE HORSE SHOW

Hector Horse worked hard on the farm. He pulled the big farm wagons. He cleared away fallen trees. But best of all, Hector liked pulling the plough!

One day, the vet came to see the farm animals. He saw Hector pulling the plough. 'What a fine horse!' he said. 'Why not enter him in the Horse Show?'

'Ooh!' cried Pam the farm girl. 'Can we do that?'

'Yes!' said the farmer. 'But, Pam...'

But Pam was already making plans for the show! 'You must have some ribbons, Hector!' she said. 'I shall plait your tail, and tie bells on your harness!'

Hector gave a loud snort. But Pam put his tail in a plait. She tied bows in his mane and bells on his harness. She was so proud as she led him along, his big hoofs clip-clopping all the way to the show.

'What a fine horse!' everyone said. But Hector did not feel so proud.

'Hello, Hector!' greeted the vet.

'Why are you wearing these fine bows and ribbons and bells?'

'You wanted Hector to enter the Horse Show!' Pam told him. 'This is what show-horses look like!'

'Not for the ploughing contest!' said the vet. He began to take off the bows, the ribbons and bells. 'Come on, Hector! Let us see what a big, strong horse you are!'

After that, Hector won the ploughing contest easily!

'Well done, Hector!' said Pam, proudly. 'What a fine horse you are!'

READ THESE WORDS AGAIN!

worked	pulled
animals	already
bows	ribbons
bells	tail
loud	proud
hoofs	greeted
contest	began

WHAT CAN YOU SEE HERE?

plough

wagon

harness

farm girl

ribbon

JACK-IN-THE-BOX KNOCKS!

Jack-in-the-Box was inside his box!
'Let me out!' he shouted.

Clown undid the catch. Then –
boing! Up jumped Jack!

'Waah!' cried Baby Bear. 'He makes
me jump!'

'Whee!' squeaked Clockwork Mouse.
'He makes me squeal!'

'Whooo!' went Spinning Top. 'He
makes me hum!'

'Back inside the box, Jack!' said
Clown. 'You frighten the toys!'

Poor Jack! Clown did feel sad.

He tapped on the box. 'Jack!' he called. 'Are you all right?'

'Yes!' shouted Jack-in-the-Box.

Clown did not hear him. 'Jack!' he shouted again. 'Are you all right?'

'Yes!' shouted Jack again.

Still Clown did not hear. 'Jack!' he shouted. 'Are you all right?'

'Is Clown talking to himself?' asked Spaceman. 'We must find out!' So the toys went closer.

'Jack!' Clown shouted again. He knocked on the box. Jack knocked back. Knock! Knock!

'Jack knocks!' said Clown. 'Out of the box!' He undid the catch and out jumped Jack-in-the-Box!

All the toys cheered!

'Again!' cried Baby Bear. 'Do it again!' So back went Jack into the box. Then – Knock! Knock!

'Jack knocks!' cried Clown. 'Out of the box!' And up jumped Jack.

Now, all the toys like hearing Jack knock. 'Jack knocks! Out of the box!' they cry. And up jumps Jack-in-the-Box.

BOING!

READ THESE WORDS AGAIN!

inside   box
knocks   undid
catch   jumped
frighten   right
shouted   closer
again   cheered
hearing   cry

WHAT CAN YOU SEE HERE?

Jack-in-the-Box

Baby Bear

Clockwork
Mouse

Spinning Top

Clown

PIXIE THE PUPPY

Pixie Puppy was a mucky pup! He splashed through mud. He padded through the dirt. He dashed through all the muck and mess.

'That Pixie Puppy!' cried the farmer's wife. 'Just look at his muddy paw-marks all over my yard!'

'Dinky Dog!' she called. 'Can you find Pixie? He needs a bath!'

Pixie squeezed through the hedge! He DID not want a bath! Off he went to hide in the stables.

Hector Horse did not see Pixie.

But he heard Dinky barking.

'Hector! Have you seen Pixie Puppy? He needs a bath!'

But Pixie had already jumped through the window. He did NOT want a bath! Off he went to hide in the cowshed.

Pixie was still panting when he heard Hector call out to the cows. 'Cora! Clara! Have you seen Pixie Puppy? He needs a bath!'

Pixie dashed through the door. He did not WANT a bath! Off he went to hide in the barn.

Just as Pixie crept inside, he heard Cora's voice. 'Donny Donkey! Have you seen Pixie Puppy? He really needs a bath!'

Pixie dashed through the door. He did not want a BATH! He wanted to hide somewhere that nobody would think of looking!

He ran into the house. Outside, voices cried, 'WHERE is Pixie Puppy? He needs a bath!' But Pixie was settling down inside a nice, warm bathroom! 'No,' he said. 'They will NEVER find me here!'

READ THESE WORDS AGAIN!

mucky · splashed
through · padded
dashed · squeezed
crept · heard
wanted · somewhere
nobody · looking
voices · warm

WHAT CAN YOU SEE HERE?

paw-marks

yard

Pixie Puppy

bath

hedge

THE STAR OF THE SHOW

'We are putting on a special show!' said Pinky Pig. 'And we are going to have a special star! Will you help us, Rag Doll?'

'Ooh, yes!' said Rag Doll.

Rag Doll draped the puppet theatre with green paper. She threaded green creepers on string. She put lots of sand on the stage. She was looking forward to the special show. She might even meet the star!

She looked around at the theatre.

It seemed to shimmer, like waves in an underwater cave.

'Oh...' said Rag Doll in wonder. She touched a coloured fish. Its tail waved, making the green creepers ripple. 'It is like magic!'

Something was shining in the sand.

'A treasure chest!' breathed Rag Doll. She lifted the lid. 'Beads! A bracelet to go on my wrist! And a crown for my head!'

Rag Doll gazed all around. 'What a lovely place,' she said.

The green creepers rippled again.

'It is like a dream...'

There was another sound. It was the sound of clapping!

'What a lovely show!' said Fairy. 'All about a princess finding her crown among the treasure!'

'Princess?' gasped Rag Doll. 'Crown? Treasure?' She turned this way and that, looking around for Pinky Pig. 'But, Pinky, what about the special show?'

'It WAS a special show!' said Pinky. 'Because YOU were the star of the show, Rag Doll!'

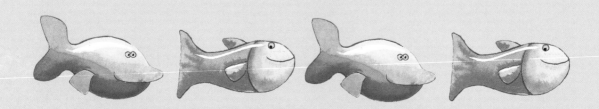

READ THESE WORDS AGAIN!

putting   special

show   draped

paper   string

stage   even

shimmer   touched

ripple   shining

bracelet   wrist

clapping   because

WHAT CAN YOU SEE HERE?

green creepers

Rag Doll

puppet theatre

coloured fish

SOMETHING LUCKY

One evening, just as supper was ending, Pixie Puppy and Dinky Dog began to bark. 'Woof-Woof!'

'What is it?' said the farmer. 'Someone trying to steal sheep?' He went out and looked around.

'The animals are quiet,' he said at last. 'But, Dinky and Pixie must have heard something!'

Next day, Brad and Mary found a hole in the hedge. 'Someone has been here,' said the farmer. 'It is near the sheep pen, too.'

'No sheep are missing!' said Sam the shepherd. 'I have just checked.'

The next strange thing was a lot of holes in the vegetable patch and a line of carrot-tops out in the lane! Here, they found a little pony, with scratches on its back and sores on its legs.

'Poor little pony!' said the farmer. 'It looks as if someone has just turned him loose. Go and ask Mum to mix some bran mash, Mary.'

'And I will fetch some water for it to drink,' said Brad.

The pony ate a dish of bran mash and drank the water. Then Mary and Brad led it into the meadow.

'I shall ask the vet to give him a check-up,' said the farmer. 'But I think he will be all right. It was lucky for him that he found us!'

'Lucky for us, too!' said Brad.

'That can be his name!' cried Mary. 'Lucky the Pony!'

Lucky stepped close to Mary and nodded his head. Then he nuzzled Brad's hand, just to show that he already felt at home on the farm!

READ THESE WORDS AGAIN!

evening	supper
steal	heard
hole	hedge
checked	found
scratches	sores
loose	bran
mash	lucky

WHAT CAN YOU SEE HERE?

vet

sheep pen

vegetable patch

carrot-tops

animals

CLOWN AND THE TOY TRAIN

Clown said his hat was magic!

'I take this ball!' he said. 'And I say – Under my hat! Er, Er…' Clown was never sure what to say! 'Er.. I do it like that!' He lifted the hat. But the ball was still there!

'Put your hat on!' said Robot. 'It is your turn to work the toy train! Push the joystick to make it go forward. Pull to make it stop!'

'Pull to go forward,' said Clown. 'Or is it, push?' He pushed so hard that his hat fell off!

It fell over the joystick! 'Under the hat!' he cried. 'Just like that!'

'Aaaagh!' Clown heard yells.

He lifted up his hat – but the joystick had gone! So had the train!

'Aaaagh!' screamed the toys. 'Where are we going?' On and on went the train, shaking and rattling, with cobwebs swaying in the darkness, ugly faces grinning and long fingers clawing at them.

'Aaaagh!' The yells came again.

'Please magic hat!' cried Clown. 'Make the toy train come back!'

It did not sound like magic. But it worked! When Clown looked, the joystick was back under the hat!

He pulled hard. There was a cloud of dust and a screech of wheels, and the train skidded to a stop on the floor! The toys got off, trembling.

'Well,' said Spaceman. 'What a BRILLIANT train ride!'

'It was!' cried the toys. 'Can we have another ride, Clown?'

But Clown had gone to have a rest. The magic train ride had been just a bit too scary for him!

READ THESE WORDS AGAIN!

magic	under
never	sure
lifted	forward
pushed	sound
screech	wheels
cloud	trembling
brilliant	scary

WHAT CAN YOU SEE HERE?

hat

joystick

Clown

cobwebs

toy train

THANK YOU, TRACTOR

Joey was the pet rabbit at Brad and Mary's school. They were looking after it over the holidays.

'He hates the noise of Dad's new tractor!' said Mary. 'Never mind, Joey! You are safe with us.'

But next day, when Brad and Mary went out into the yard, the hutch was open! Joey had gone!

'A fox has gnawed the latch on the hutch!' said their dad. 'Now we shall have lots of wild rabbits running all over the farm!'

'We will find him!' said Mary. 'Fetch the pet carrier, Brad!'

But there was no sign of Joey.

'That noisy tractor!' said Mary. 'How can Joey hear us calling?'

Suddenly the noise stopped. 'Come on, tractor!' said the farmer. He turned the key to start the engine, but the tractor did not go.

Then, Brad and Mary saw a little, white, fluffy tail. 'Joey!' they cried. 'He is under the tractor!'

'Stay where you are!' called their dad 'Give me the pet carrier!'

'Joey's nose is twitching!' said Brad. 'He is coming out!'

They held their breath. Joey went into the pet carrier and their dad closed the door. 'Keep him in this until I mend the hutch!' he said. 'Now let me see to this tractor!'

He went to the tractor, got into the driver's seat and turned the key. And, the tractor started up as if nothing had happened!

'Look!' said Mary. 'When Joey was under the tractor, it did not budge! Thank you, tractor!'

READ THESE WORDS AGAIN!

school   holidays
gnawed   wild
fetch   noisy
turned   key
engine   under
called   give
twitching   budge

WHAT CAN YOU SEE HERE?

tractor

hutch

rabbit

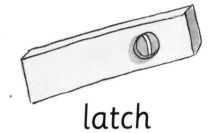

latch

pet carrier

NO RUST FOR ROBOT!

The bath-toys were in the sink having lots of fun! 'Quack!' went Duck, splashing water.

'Whirr!' went the boat, chasing bubbles.

'Whee!' went Whale, flapping his flippers. 'MUST you be so noisy?' said Rag Doll. 'Robot is not well!'

'It is a touch of rust,' said Robot. 'Rust makes me stiff and clanky.'

'Have a rest in the wendy house,' said Fairy. 'And DO be quiet, bath-toys! Just for a little while!'

'Wheee!' went Whale. 'I shall make some soapy bubbles!' But, as he reached for the soap, it shot out of his flippers and on to the floor!

BUMP! Down went Robot, slipping and sliding on the soap!

'Poor Robot!' said Fairy. 'Can you move? Can you get up?'

'I do not think so,' said Robot.

'Be careful,' said Rag Doll. 'You are lying on the soap!'

The toys tried moving Robot, first one way and then the other. But he was too heavy.

Next, they tried lifting Robot, first one way and then the other.

'Do try to move, Robot!' said Blue Rabbit. 'Just a little bit!'

'I am so stiff,' Robot began. Then he stopped. 'My rusty arm!' he cried. 'I can move it! It is not sore!'

'That arm is COVERED in dirty soap!' said Fairy. 'What a mess!'

'Wheee!' cried Whale. 'The soap got rid of the rust! Robot will not feel stiff and clanky now!'

'No!' cried Robot. 'I feel like a new robot!'

READ THESE WORDS AGAIN!

quack   splashing
water   flippers
noisy   stiff
clanky   quiet
little   while
sliding   careful
heavy   first

WHAT CAN YOU SEE HERE?

soapy
bubbles

Robot

Whale

rusty arm

sink

COPY-CAT CLARA COW

Clara Cow liked to be just the same as Cora Cow. If Cora went into the meadow, so did Clara. If Cora had a nap, Clara had a nap.

'Moo!' went Cora Cow.

'Moo!' went Clara Cow.

'You are a copy-cat, Clara!' mooed Cora. 'You copy everything I do!'

'Clara just wants to be like you, Cora!' said the farmer. 'There is no harm in that!' He held up two cowbells, each tied on a ribbon.

'A bell for you, Cora!' he said. 'And one for you, Clara!'

Clara was very pleased. Cora was very cross!

'You will each have a calf soon!' said the farmer. 'Maybe Clara will have her calf on the same day as you, Cora!'

This made Cora feel even more cross! 'Why must Clara copy me all the time?' she said to herself. 'I hope Clara has her calf first! Then she cannot copy me!'

But Cora was the first cow to have her calf. 'What a fine calf!' said the farmer.

'Moo!' went Cora, very loudly indeed. 'Look again!'

So he looked again. And there, just getting up on its wobbly legs was a second calf, just the same as the first!

'Twin calves!' cried the farmer. 'Well done, Cora!' He was very pleased. But not as pleased as Cora!

'Twin calves!' she mooed. 'Clara Cow cannot copy THAT!'

READ THESE WORDS AGAIN!

meadow   mooed
copy   everything
harm   ribbon
pleased   cross
first   cannot
loudly   indeed
wobbly   second

WHAT CAN YOU SEE HERE?

cowbells

cow

farmer

twin calves

calf

A SURPRISE FOR ROCKING HORSE

Rocking Horse had lived in the playroom for a long time. He liked giving rides, telling stories and just being with his friends.

One day, Dolly came hurrying past.

'Why all the hurry?' he called. 'What is the matter?'

'I cannot stop!' she said. And she went into the Wendy House.

Rocking Horse was puzzled.

'What is going on?' he asked Fairy. 'Dolly always likes a chat!'

'I cannot stop!' said Fairy.

She flew into the Wendy House!

'What IS going on?' said Rocking Horse again. 'Puppets, come and tell me!'

'We cannot stop!' said the puppets. And they went into the Wendy House, too!

One by one, all the toys hurried past. Rocking Horse was very upset. Why had he been left on his own? What was going on?

Still feeling sad and alone, he fell asleep. In his dreams, he felt a blanket being put on his back.

Then, he heard the voices of friends.
'Wake up, Rocking Horse!'

So Rocking Horse woke up. And there he was, with all his friends, a new blanket on his back, and a puppet show about to begin!

'Surprise, surprise!' said the toys.

'You are so nice to us, Rocking Horse!' said Cat. 'We wanted to do something nice for you!'

'Something nice?' said Rocking Horse. 'This is more than something nice! It – it is the most WONDERFUL surprise!'

READ THESE WORDS AGAIN!

lived   hurrying
past   matter
puzzled   chat
cannot   stop
alone   dreams
around   voices
something   surprise

WHAT CAN YOU SEE HERE?

Wendy House

puppets

Rocking Horse

friends

blanket

KITTY CAT AND KITTEN

No cat was better than Kitty at catching mice, chasing rats – or teaching Kitten to be a farm cat!

One day, as Kitty was helping Hetty Hen to get the chicks back into the henhouse, she saw a mouse.

'Chase that mouse away from the house!' she hissed at Kitten.

Kitten dashed forward. But Dinky Dog had seen the mouse too. 'Woof-woof!' Her barks scared Kitten.

With a loud 'MIAOW!' she jumped up into a tree.

'Woof!' barked Dinky. 'I did not mean to scare you! Come down, Kitten!' She jumped up at the tree. But Kitten climbed even higher.

'Come down, Kitten!' mewed Kitty. She began to climb the tree. But Kitten climbed even higher.

Brad came along with Hector Horse.

'Kitten!' he cried. 'Jump down on Hector's back!' But Kitten climbed even higher.

'I know!' cried Mary. She went to get some fish and milk. 'Here, Kitten!' she called. 'Come down!'

Kitten stopped. She looked down. Then a bundle of fur and a fluffy tail streaked down the tree and Kitten jumped to the ground!

'Good Kitten!' cried Brad. 'You saw the food Mary got for you!'

But Kitten did not look at the food! She was getting a lost chick into the henhouse, just like Kitty!

'THAT is why Kitten came down!' said Mary. 'Because she saw that chick! Clever Kitten!'

And Kitty stroked her whiskers to show that she quite agreed.

READ THESE WORDS AGAIN!

better   catching
chasing   teaching
hissed   dashed
scared   climbed
even   higher
know   bundle
fluffy   because

142

WHAT CAN YOU SEE HERE?

Kitty Cat

mouse

Kitten

mice

whiskers

DOLLY'S THREE WISHES

Fairy liked being with all the toys. 'I did not like being with the Christmas decorations!' she told Dolly. 'I like being here!'

'Good!' said Dolly. 'Is that really a magic wand in your hand?'

'Yes!' smiled Fairy. 'I can grant three wishes, just by waving it! Make a wish, Dolly!'

'Ooh!' said Dolly. 'I DO I wish I had wings like yours, Fairy!' So Fairy waved her wand – and there was Dolly with silver wings!

'Ooh!' she cried. 'Thank you very much, Fairy!'

'Look at me!' cried Dolly, as she flapped her wings and flew and fluttered around. 'Look at my wings!'

The toys smiled. Dolly did look very funny!

'You will need to rest soon,' said Blue Rabbit. 'You look tired!'

Dolly WAS tired. But when she sat in a chair, her wings dug into her back. She tried to lie down. But her wings got in the way.

Then she tried to rest on a stool.

But she kept falling off! Dolly was in tears.

'Oh, dear!' said Fairy. 'Poor Dolly! You do not like your wings, do you?'

'No,' sobbed Dolly. 'Fairy, can I wish to be just the way I was?'

So Fairy waved her magic wand – and the wings had gone.

'Thank you, Fairy!' said Dolly. 'I am myself again!'

'One more wish, Dolly!' said Fairy. 'What is it to be?'

'I wish for us all to be happy,' said Dolly. 'Just as we are!'

READ THESE WORDS AGAIN!

wish   decorations

like   three

grant   smiled

flapped   flew

fluttered   chair

stool   falling

myself   happy

WHAT CAN YOU SEE HERE?

Fairy

wings

magic wand

Dolly

toys

THE NEW BEAST

The farmer was talking to Brad and Mary. 'I want to find a real beast! We need him in the cornfield!'

'A beast?' said Hector Horse. 'That means an animal.'

'YOU are a strong beast!' said Donny Donkey. 'You work hard in the cornfield, too! Surely, another animal is not taking your place?'

'We will not LET another animal take your place,' said Dinky Dog.

But Brad and Mary were busy, getting everything ready!

'We need hay to make him nice and fat,' said Mary.

'Not OUR nice hay!' said Donny. He kicked at a haystack. A heap of hard, dry hay fell to the ground. But Brad was pleased!

'Thanks, Donny!' he cried. 'Now, he needs some wool!'

'Not MY wool!' said Letty Lamb. She found some scraps of wet, dirty wool. But Mary was pleased!

'Thanks, Letty!' she cried. 'Now he needs a turnip!'

'Not a NICE turnip!' said Dinky.

She dug up such a soggy turnip! But Brad and Mary were pleased!

'Everything is ready!' said Mary. 'Soon, everybody will see him in the cornfield!'

One by one, the animals went to the cornfield. The farmer sounded VERY pleased!

'WHAT a beast he looks!' he said 'Sammy, the scarecrow!'

'He is keeping the crows away!' cried Brad. 'They HATE him!'

'Yes,' smiled Mary. 'But you can see the animals LOVE him!'

READ THESE WORDS AGAIN!

talking	beast
animal	surely
another	busy
ready	kicked
scraps	wool
pleased	soggy
sounded	what

WHAT CAN YOU SEE HERE?

crows

scarecrow

haystack

cornfield

turnip

THE LOST SQUEAK

Squeaky Snake had lost his squeak!

Robot banged him on the back. Fairy squeezed him tight. But his squeak had not come back.

Sadly, Squeaky wandered about. Suddenly he heard the thump of big feet. He looked up to see two tusks and a long, grey trunk among the thick, green plants.

'Am I in the jungle?' gasped Squeaky.

'A balcony is as good as a jungle for an elephant without a trumpet noise,' came a voice.

'A trumpet noise?' said Squeaky. 'Was it like this?' He blew on a whistle. A tinny sound came out.

'No,' smiled Elephant. 'That is not like my trumpet noise.'

'Was it like this?' said Squeaky. He blew on a bubble-pipe. A bubbly sound came out.

'No,' Elephant smiled again. 'That is not like my trumpet noise!'

'Was it like this?' said Squeaky. He took a balloon and blew and blew until – BANG! The balloon burst! And Squeaky gave a squeak!

'SQUEAK! My squeak is back!' he cried. 'Squeak! SQUEAK!'

But, Elephant was laughing too much to listen! 'Ha-ha! HA-HA!' Then, 'Tara-Tara! TARA-TARA!'

'SQUEAK!' went Squeaky. 'You have got your trumpet noise back!'

'TARA-TARA!' went Elephant.

'You have got your squeak back!'

Now, just to make sure that Squeaky can squeak and Elephant can make a trumpet noise, they make each other laugh! SQUEAK-SQUEAK! TARA-TARA!

READ THESE WORDS AGAIN!

squeak	banged
squeezed	tight
wandered	thump
tusks	trunk
noise	voice
sound	bubbly
blew	burst
laughing	listen

WHAT CAN YOU SEE HERE?

Elephant

balcony

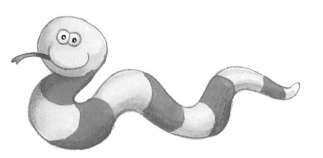

Squeaky Snake

whistle

bubble-pipe

SHEP THE SHEEPDOG

Shep was learning to be a sheepdog. His job was to help Sam the shepherd care for the sheep. But Shep was not good at his job!

'Shep!' cried Sam. 'Do not jump around. That frightens the sheep!'

'Woof!' Shep barked. That made the sheep jump in fright! 'Woof!'

One day, Shep saw a big bird swooping down. 'Woof!' he barked and chased it across the stream. He did not think about the sheep following him!

Then Shep got out and shook himself. Drops of water went all over the sheep. They all ran off.

'Maybe Shep will never make a sheepdog, Sam!' said the farmer.

'But he is a good dog,' said Sam. 'I shall give him one last try.'

Shep heard what Sam said. If only he could show Sam that he could make a good sheepdog!

Just then, his ears pricked up.

'Baa! Baa!' It was a sound Shep knew. 'Baa! Baa!'

Shep squeezed under a hedge.

He ran through a muddy cabbage patch, across the yard and along a path. 'Baa! Baa!' Two sheep had fallen into a ditch!

'Woof!' Shep crouched down beside the ditch, to show that he was taking care of the sheep.

'Shep!' came Sam's voice. 'Your muddy paw prints led me here!'

'Woof!' Shep barked back.

'Silly sheep!' said Sam. He got them out of the ditch. 'Go on, Shep, see them home, boy! I can see you are a sheepdog, now!'

READ THESE WORDS AGAIN!

learning   help

fright   swooping

barked   following

water   heard

could   squeezed

hedge   across

fallen   prints

WHAT CAN YOU SEE HERE?

sheep

shepherd

big bird

hedge

prints

KITE AT THE SEASIDE

Kite had been to so many places! High up in the sky on his long string, he had seen green fields and wide rivers and busy roads. Best of all, Kite liked the seaside!

'I just cannot describe it!' he told the toys. 'There is so much to see at the seaside!'

'Maybe,' said Fluffy Cat. 'But none of us will ever see it!'

'What is the seaside like?' asked Clown. 'Can you tell us, Kite?'

Kite looked around.

'That tin tray!' he said. 'The sea is like that, smooth and shiny!'

'Put it on the floor!' said Clown. So that is what the toys did.

'Put some bricks on top!' said Kite. 'They can be toy boats!' So that is what the toys did.

'We need a sandy beach!' Kite went on. 'That bit of brown paper at the bottom of the cupboard! Put it on the floor!' So that is what the toys did.

Then Dolly opened her pink umbrella and put it on the beach.

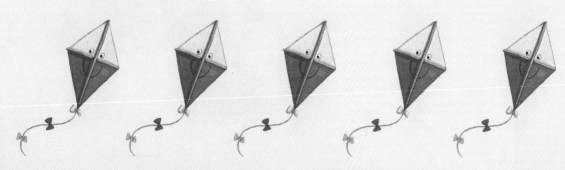

'Now we need pebbles to play with!'
said Kite. He looked around again.
'Those bits of jigsaw puzzle can be
pebbles! Put them in a heap on the
beach! Now we are all at our very
own seaside!'

And so they were. Dolly and Fairy
sat under the beach umbrella. Blue
Rabbit and Clown sailed boats on the
sea. Fluffy Cat and Rag Doll played
with the pebbles. And, Kite? High up
on his long string, he just liked being
at the seaside!

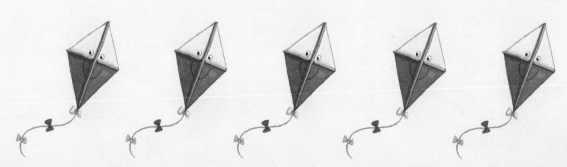

READ THESE WORDS AGAIN!

high	sky
string	describe
none	smooth
shiny	bricks
boats	sandy
cupboard	floor
beach	umbrella

WHAT CAN YOU SEE HERE?

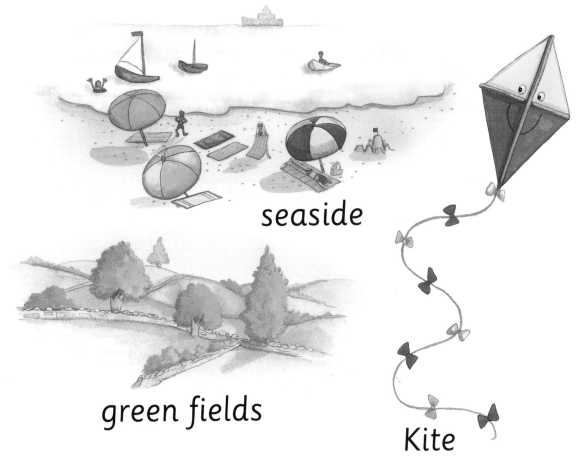

seaside

green fields

Kite

pebbles

bits of jigsaw puzzle

183

THE OLD CARAVAN

There was an old caravan on the farm. It was shabby and broken, but Mary and Brad loved it.

'That old caravan!' said Mum one day. 'It could fall to bits!'

'These winds could blow it over!' said Dad. 'We should break it up!'

'No!' cried Mary and Brad. 'No!'

'All right,' said the farmer. 'I will look at it tomorrow.'

But that night, the winds blew stronger, ripping tiles from the roof and blowing down fences.

It made the caravan rock about so much that its front wheels had broken! What would happen, now?

'Our henhouse was damaged, too!' said Mum. 'All the hens and the chicks have run away!'

Later, Brad and Mary went outside.

'Stay away from the caravan,' said Mum. 'It is too dangerous!'

'All right,' said Brad. 'We will help look for the hens instead.'

They looked in the barn, under the hedges and in the stables. The hens were nowhere to be found.

'Look, Brad!' said Mary. 'Look at our caravan!' They looked. Then they heard clucking! And a fluffy brown head poked out of the window!

'The hens!' cried Brad. 'We must go and tell Dad!' So they did.

'Our hens are safe!' said the farmer. 'The broken wheels made the caravan lower, so they could get inside! Now we could take all the wheels off, to make it safe!'

Brad and Mary cheered! And the hens went on clucking, just to show they loved the caravan, too!

READ THESE WORDS AGAIN!

shabby	broken
could	should
right	tomorrow
night	stronger
ripping	damaged
dangerous	instead
nowhere	fluffy

WHAT CAN YOU SEE HERE?

fence

wheel

old caravan

henhouse

stables

FLUFFY CAT'S LUCKY CHARM

One day, Fluffy Cat found something on the floor. It was round and red, with a hole in the middle. 'What a pretty bead!' she said. 'It can be my lucky charm!'

Fluffy Cat went to pick the bead up, but it rolled into a mouse hole. She reached inside, and – ouch! – she scraped her paw! It did hurt!

'Never mind!' she said. 'I still have my lucky charm!'

But even as Fluffy Cat spoke, the bead slipped from her paw.

'Never mind!' said Fluffy Cat. 'I can soon pick it up!'

She bent down, and – BUMP! – she bumped her head on the windowsill! It did hurt!

'Never mind,' she said. 'I still have my lucky charm!'

She held the bead tightly. But it still slipped from her paw and rolled under a pile of puzzles!

'Never mind,' said Fluffy Cat. 'I can soon pick it up!'

She bent down, and – CRASH! – down fell the puzzles!

'Fluffy Cat!' cried Dolly. 'What ARE you doing?'

'Picking up my lucky charm!' said Fluffy Cat. 'But this red bead has not been very lucky so far! Ooh, my poor head! My sore paw!'

'Red bead?' said Dolly. 'It is the wheel that the wooden horse lost! We have all been looking for it!'

'Never mind, Fluffy Cat!' smiled Robot. 'The little wheel may not have been lucky for you, but it was lucky for the wooden horse that you found it!'

READ THESE WORDS AGAIN!

round　　　　hole
middle　　　pretty
rolled　　　scraped
never　　　 mind
tightly　　　pile
little　　　　lost
looking　　 found

WHAT CAN YOU SEE HERE?

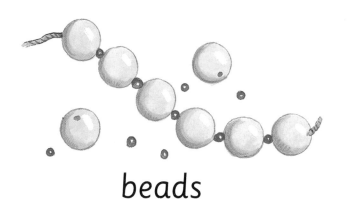

beads

lucky charms

mouse hole

paw

puzzles

PIGEONS TO THE RESCUE!

Brad and Mary were at an old windmill with Pam, the stable-girl. Once, the mill had ground corn to make flour. It had been empty for a long time, but Pam's Dad hoped to get it working again.

'Then we can use fresh flour in the bakery next door!' he said. 'Now, I must inspect the roof!'

'Take care, Dad,' said Pam. 'Come on, kids, time to go home!'

As they went outside, there was a loud flutter of wings.

'Sam's racing pigeons!' said Pam. 'They are flying back home!'

They saw Sam the shepherd as Pam drove the jeep into the yard.

'Sam!' said Brad. 'We saw your pigeons near the old windmill!'

'But my pigeons are not back!' said Sam. 'Where have they gone?'

They went to Sam's pigeon loft, at the top of an old barn. They waited and waited. Then, there was a flutter of wings. In flew a pigeon and perched on a ledge. On its leg there was a note.

The note read:

PLEASE HELP. I AM ON A LEDGE IN THE OLD MILL. PAM'S DAD.

Sam called the fire service! Before long, firemen had put up a long ladder to reach Pam's Dad.

'I was near the roof and some of the steps crumbled away!' he said. 'Thank goodness I got Sam's pigeon to carry a message!'

'It did not win a race,' said Brad.

'There will be other races,' said Sam. 'Just as long as they do not stop at the windmill too often!'

READ THESE WORDS AGAIN!

ground   flour
fresh   loud
outside   flutter
wings   racing
loft   waited
perched   ledge
note   firemen

WHAT CAN YOU SEE HERE?

old windmill

flour

bakery

pigeons

jeep

MONSTER MOUSE

Clockwork Mouse hated not being seen by the other toys!

'Nearly trod on your tail!' said Robot. 'I did not see you!'

'Sorry I bumped into you!' said Spinning Top. 'I did not see you!'

'Sorry I did not say hello!' said Blue Rabbit. 'I did not see you!'

One day, Clockwork Mouse found a mask. He put his wheels inside and it flipped up in front of him. What an ugly monster face!

'Help!' cried Dolly. 'A monster!'

Clockwork Mouse gave a little squeak. The toys were sure to see him now! He tried a monster voice.

'Whooo! I am a monster!'

'Help!' wailed Blue Rabbit. 'There is a monster in here!'

'Whooo!' went Clockwork Mouse again. 'I am a monster!'

'Help!' screamed Baby Bear. 'There is a monster in here!'

He sounded so frightened that Clockwork Mouse felt mean.

'Wait!' he cried. He tried to get out of the mask, but he couldn't.

He was wedged tightly inside.

'A monster!' cried Fairy. 'Help!'

Clockwork Mouse wriggled. He jiggled. Then he pulled. Off came the mask. Robot spoke first.

'Some monster! Clockwork Mouse and a monster mask!'

'Sorry if I frightened you,' said Clockwork Mouse. 'But I wanted to be seen!' He looked so sorry for himself that the toys smiled.

'Well,' said Clown, 'it is nice to know that there is not a REAL monster in here, after all!'

READ THESE WORDS AGAIN!

hated	sorry
bumped	hello
wheels	flipped
front	ugly
help	squeak
frightened	mean
himself	real

WHAT CAN YOU SEE HERE?

tail

monster mask

Clockwork
Mouse

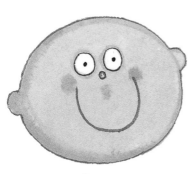

face

Blue Rabbit

215

DOWN BY THE LAKE

'Pam!' Sam the shepherd called to the stable-girl. 'A fence has blown down by the lake!'

Letty Lamb heard him. 'Cora Cow!' she cried. 'I have some important news!'

'Important news?' said Cora. 'What is it?'

Letty tried to think. 'Er, there are grown men down by the lake!'

Soon, Cora saw Donny Donkey.

'Donny!' she cried. 'I have some important news!'

'Important news?' said Donny. 'What is it?'

Cora tried to think. 'Er, a brown hen went round by the lake!'

'What news!' said Donny.

'Dinky Dog!' cried Donny. 'I have some important news!'

'Important news?' said Dinky Dog. 'What is it?'

Donny tried to think. 'Er... a man lost a pen by the lake!'

'What?' barked Dinky. She ran all the way to the lake. 'Where is Sly Fox and his den?' she panted.

'Sly Fox and his den?' said Donny. 'You mean, a lost pen!'

'Lost pen?' mooed Cora. 'You mean a brown hen!'

'Brown hen?' bleated Letty Lamb. 'You mean, grown men!'

'Sly fox?' said Sam. 'Lost pen? Brown hen? Grown men? A fence has blown down by the lake!'

The animals looked at each other.

'That is JUST what we were saying!' said Letty.

'Good!' said Sam. 'You can all help us to mend it!'

READ THESE WORDS AGAIN!

called	blown
important	news
grown	tried
soon	think
panted	donkey
bleated	looked
were	saying
good	all

WHAT CAN YOU SEE HERE?

fence

brown hen

lake

stable-girl

animals

PIGGY BANK'S JINGLE

'Oh, dear!' said Piggy Bank one day. 'I DO miss my jingle!'

'Your jingle?' said Robot. He was tidying the playroom. 'What do you mean, your jingle?'

'People used to put money in my slot!' Piggy Bank explained. 'The coins made a LOVELY jingle!'

'Now,' he added sadly, 'I am empty. So my jingle has gone.'

'What a shame!' said Robot. He went to pick up a counter off the floor and a dial fell off his control panel!

'What a shame!' said Robot. 'Where can I put this?'

He saw the slot in Piggy Bank's back. 'That is an idea!' he said. And he put the dial in the slot. It made Piggy Bank jingle! Then Robot put in the counter. Piggy Bank jingled again, even louder. Fairy heard him.

'That is an idea!' cried Fairy. 'I shall put this bead from my crown in Piggy Bank's slot!'

'And this safety pin!' said Rag Doll. 'And this hairgrip!' She put them in Piggy Bank's slot.

Piggy Bank jingled again!

'This brass stud has come off my harness!' said Rocking-Horse. 'Put it in Piggy Bank's slot, please!'

'And my spare key!' said Clockwork Mouse.

'And this button!' said Dolly.

A badge, a tag, a ring, a nail – so many things went into Piggy Bank's slot! How glad he was to get his jingle back! And how glad the toys were for Piggy Bank to keep all the things safely until they needed them.

Jingle! Jingle!

READ THESE WORDS AGAIN!

jingle   people
money   coins
explained   empty
shame   counter
floor   slot
idea   louder
harness   key
things   needed

WHAT CAN YOU SEE HERE?

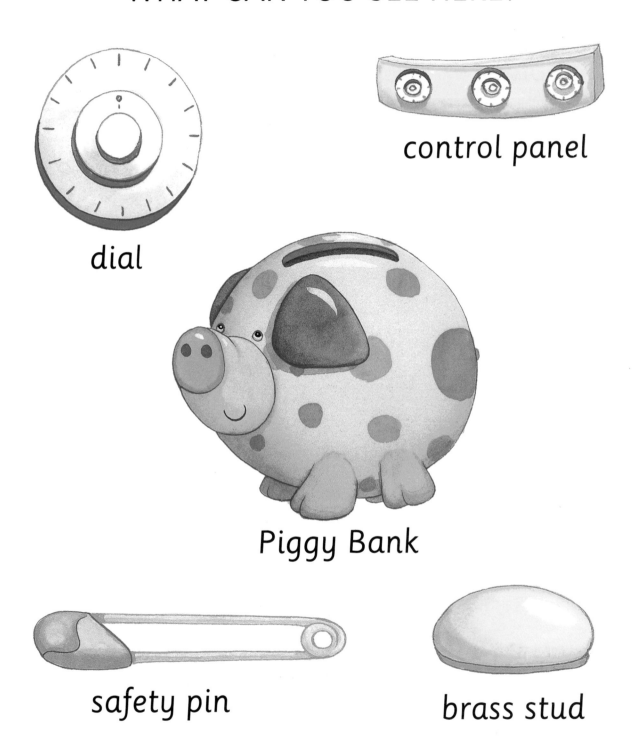

dial

control panel

Piggy Bank

safety pin

brass stud

HAYSTACK HUNT

'I put it in my pocket!' The farmer sounded cross about something! 'Where CAN it be?'

'It is like looking for a needle in a haystack!' said his wife.

'You are right,' said the farmer. 'A needle in a haystack...'

'A needle!' said Donny Donkey. 'So that is what the farmer has lost!'

'He must have lost it in that big haystack!' said Guppy Goat. 'Let us look!' So they looked all around the big haystack.

Then Donny scrabbled with his hoofs and made the hay fly about. But there was no needle.

Guppy dug into the haystack with his horns. Bits of hay flew about. There was no needle. But there was an untidy heap of hay where the haystack had been!

'We must find the needle soon!' Donny panted. 'Then just think how pleased the farmer will be!'

The farmer did not look pleased!

'What have you done to my haystack?' he roared. 'Look...'

He bent down to pick something up.

'The key to my tractor!' he cried. 'It must have fallen out of my pocket at hay-making!'

Donny and Guppy looked at each other. 'Farmer was cross,' said Donny. 'Then he was pleased.'

'It was not a needle he lost,' said Guppy, 'but a key.'

'And the key was not to open a door,' said Donny, 'but a tractor!'

'It is such a puzzle,' said Guppy at last. 'We need a feed of hay to help us work it out!'

READ THESE WORDS AGAIN!

pocket	sounded
cross	something
donkey	goat
scrabbled	hoofs
horns	untidy
panted	pleased
roared	puzzle

WHAT CAN YOU SEE HERE?

pocket

needle

haystack

tractor

key

SPACEMAN AND BABY BEAR

Spaceman was at the window, looking out at the night sky.

'I do not like night-time!' said Baby Bear. 'I hate the dark.'

'The night is not ALL dark!' said Spaceman. 'Come and see how brightly the moon shines!'

So Baby Bear went to the window. 'Those stars are so bright!' he said. 'Is that what you look at every night, Spaceman?'

'Yes,' said Spaceman. 'I hope I might see a spaceship, too!'

'What is a spaceship like?' said Baby Bear. 'Is it like a bright, shiny bubble with bright lights?'

'That is right!' said Spaceman. 'How did you know?'

'There is one right there!' cried Baby Bear, pointing. He was right!

The spaceship came closer, its lights flashing. A bright beam of light closed in around Spaceman and Baby Bear. Then, they were in the spaceship! The light from the moon and the stars made the sky as bright as day. What a fantastic sight!

'I have dreamt of this every night!' Spaceman kept saying. 'Now, it is beginning to get light. Night is coming to an end.'

As he spoke a beam of light inside the spaceship became so bright that he and Baby Bear had to close their eyes tight. When they opened them again, they were back in the house, looking out of the window!

'What a flight!' said Spaceman. 'Are you all right, Baby Bear?'

But Baby Bear was already fast asleep, dreaming of spaceships!

READ THESE WORDS AGAIN!

window	dark
brightly	shines
stars	every
might	too
shiny	lights
right	flashing
close	beginning

WHAT CAN YOU SEE HERE?

Spaceman

night sky

spaceship

Baby Bear

beam of light

OH, DINKY DOG!

Dinky Dog was always picking up bones and twigs and bits of wood and lots of other things.

'This rubbish!' said Pixie Pup. 'I just cannot get into my kennel!'

'Such a mess!' agreed Hetty Hen. 'We have no room to move!'

'But we may need this wood,' said Dinky, 'or that twig, or...'

'Or that odd boot,' said Giddy Goat. 'Or this old wheel, or...'

But Dinky had seen the farmer getting into his jeep.

That meant a ride into town!

'Woof!' she barked. 'Wait for me!'

'Now is our chance!' said Hector Horse. 'We can tidy up the yard before Dinky gets back!'

So, Pixie and Kitty Cat picked up bits of wood and twigs and straw in their mouths. Hetty and Giddy rolled away cotton reels, broken wheels and door-knobs. Hector scooped it all into an old basket ready to throw away!

'I can hear the farm jeep!' said Pixie. 'Dinky is coming back!'

The animals expected Dinky to be cross, but she sounded pleased!

'I found this basket by the gate!' she cried. 'Look what's inside!'

'But, Dinky,' began Hector, 'that is rubbish, to be thrown away!'

'There is no room to keep it!' said Pixie. But Dinky was already emptying the basket all over the clean, tidy farmyard.

'Look!' she said. 'There is plenty of room! AND I have a nice, big basket, all ready to keep lots more useful things!'

READ THESE WORDS AGAIN!

twigs

cannot

boot

picked

wheels

expected

emptying

other

room

chance

broken

scooped

basket

already